This Book belongs to

Gina D'An...

Ph...

A

Gift

From

Dr. And Mrs. George D'Angelo

to

Mercyhurst College
Hammermill Library

2008

27 CATS NEXT DOOR

27 CATS

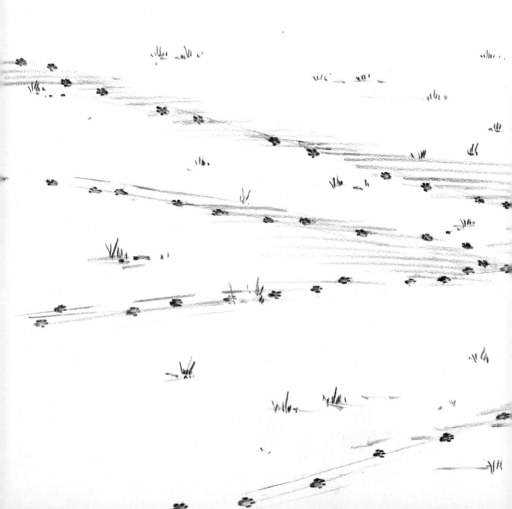

NEXT DOOR

By Anita Feagles

With Illustrations by Robert A. Shipman

YOUNG SCOTT BOOKS · NEW YORK

MERCYHURST COLLEGE
HAMMERMILL LIBRARY
ERIE, PA 16546

Library of Congress Catalog Card No. 65-12581
©1965 BY ANITA FEAGLES. ALL RIGHTS RESERVED.
Made in U.S.A.

Table of Contents

Moving to a new town wasn't nearly as bad as Jim had expected. In some ways, he was glad they'd moved. For one thing, he didn't have to share a room with his little brother, Billy, any more, because they'd moved into a bigger house. Billy was only four years old, and it was awful to share a room with him, because he was such a pain in the neck. He got into Jim's things, and he made a terrible noise sucking his thumb at night.

Another good thing about moving was that his new house was near everything. Jim could walk to the movies and the library and the drug store. When school started again in the fall, he would even be able to walk to school.

But the best thing about moving was

that Jim found two friends, Dave and Jeff. They were hanging around the yard the first day, when the movers were carrying the furniture into the house, so Jim had someone to play with from the beginning. Dave lived only a short distance down the street, Jeff lived at the end of the block, and Jim quickly learned the way to both houses. Within a few days they had explored all over town, and Jim knew where everything was. He could even tell his mother where the hardware store and the Post Office were.

There was only one trouble, and that didn't seem too important at first. It was the cat lady.

One day Jeff said, "Did you know you're living next door to a crazy lady?"

"No," Jim said.

"Yeah," Dave said. "Mrs. Ames. She's nuts. She has about eighty cats, and she wears funny clothes and never lets anyone in the house."

"That's probably because it stinks,"
Jeff said, and they all laughed.

"Wow!" Jim said. "Eighty cats! I
thought I saw quite a few cats around,
but I never thought too much of it."

"She lives all alone except for those cats," Dave said. "Everyone on the street complains about them. They howl at night, and kill the birds, and get into the garbage."

"Everyone's scared of her, too," Jeff said. "The kids don't even go there on Halloween. One time Mrs. Bolton asked her if she could use the telephone because hers wasn't working, and Mrs. Ames wouldn't even let her do that."

"Well," Jim said, "I'll bet my little brother will go there on Halloween. He goes everywhere. He'll probably bring home a few cats while he's at it."

Dave laughed. "Then your mother and father will start complaining, along with everyone else."

"Oh, don't worry," Jim said. "If it gets too bad, my Dad will do something."

That night, Jim asked his parents about the cat lady.

"The guys say that the woman next

door, Mrs. Ames, has eighty cats. Do you think that's true?"

"She certainly has a great many," Jim's mother said. "Some of them knocked the garbage can over yesterday and spread the garbage all over the grass."

"I'm surprised the law hasn't stepped in," Jim's father said. "In most towns, you're not permitted to keep more than a certain number of animals without a kennel license."

"I suppose nobody has ever bothered to report it," Jim's mother said.

"The guys say everyone on the street complains," said Jim.

"I wouldn't be surprised," Jim's father said.

Jim didn't think much about the cat lady for a while after that, but he did begin to notice the cats.

First he decided to try to count them. He didn't believe there were eighty, but he did get to recognize fifteen of them. He didn't know their names, of course, but he began making up names for the ones he saw most often. There was a kitten that got into the habit of following him around, and sometimes he sat on the back stairs and played with it. He called it Baby, because it was so little. Then there was a big old gray cat who liked to lie across one of the back steps, so that Jim had to step over him whenever he went up or down. Jim called him Lazy Grandpa. Jim would say, "Hey, Lazy Grandpa, get moving, so I can get up the steps." But Lazy Grandpa never moved, and Jim would finally bend down and scratch him behind the ears for a while before he stepped over him.

There was one cat Jim thought was beautiful. She was all white, and had long fur and blue eyes. Jim tried to think of a beautiful name for her. He remembered a girl in his first grade who had long blond hair and blue eyes and her name was Linda, so he named the beautiful cat Linda.

After he got to know several of the cats, Jim began wondering what the cat lady was really like. When he passed her house he'd look up to see if she was looking out, but she never was. There was a high, thick hedge between Jim's house and Mrs. Ames' house, and there was only one spot where he could see through a little bit. Once in a while, he'd caught sight of her working in her garden or putting out her milk bottles, but she never looked up, and he had never gotten a really good look at her.

One day, Jim was helping his mother carry the groceries in from the car. As he opened the screen door, a cat raced into the kitchen with a dog in full pursuit.

"Hey, go on home!" Jim shouted. The dog stopped at the door, looked at Jim, then turned and ran off. Jim closed the door and put the bag of groceries down.

"What was that?" his mother asked.

"Oh, some dog chased one of the cats into the house."

"Into *our* house?" asked his mother.

"Yes. I'll try to get it out," Jim said.

"Take it over to Mrs. Ames."

"Me? Why me?"

"Well, I really don't think I'd have any luck getting her to come to the door. A package of hers was delivered here by mistake one day, so I took it over to her and rang the front doorbell and then the back doorbell, but she never answered."

"Well, she must not have been home, then," Jim said.

"One of the neighbors told me she never goes out. I think she just doesn't like to see people. But she might not be as timid with a child."

"O.K., I don't mind," Jim said. "I'd like to have a look at her, anyway."

Jim didn't find the cat downstairs, so he went upstairs. As soon as he saw Billy's door closed, he knew the cat must be in there, because Billy never closed his door unless he had something he didn't want anyone to see.

"Billy, do you have a cat in there?"

"No!" Billy said. "It's my cat!"

Jim laughed and opened the door. Billy let him take the cat when he explained that it lived next door. He went outside and squeezed through the bushes. Then he knocked on Mrs. Ames' back door.

He had almost given up when the door opened, and a lady peered out.

"A dog chased one of your cats into our house," Jim said.

Mrs. Ames reached out and took the cat. "Thank you for bringing him back," she said, and closed the door. And that was that! He still hadn't had a very good look at her.

A few days later he was in his back yard, and Linda came over and rubbed up against his leg.

"Hello, Linda," he said. "One of these days I'm going fishing, and maybe I'll bring you a fish. I bet you'd like that."

"Now that's very odd," someone said.

Jim turned, and he could see that Mrs. Ames was standing on the other side of the bushes. He was a little embarrassed to be overheard talking to a cat, so he ducked his head and said, "Oh, yeah."

"It's very odd that you named her Linda," Mrs. Ames went on. "Because that's the name I gave her, too. It means 'pretty' in Spanish. Lazy Grandpa's name is really Sampson, and Baby's name is Esmeralda."

Jim was quite surprised and embarrassed that Mrs. Ames had overheard so many of his private conversations, but he couldn't help grinning at the silly names. "Oh," he said.

"What is your name?" Mrs. Ames asked.

"Jim."

"Do you like cottage cheese, Jim?"

"Cottage cheese?"

"Yes," Mrs. Ames said. "I just made some. Would you like to try it?"

Jim had never liked cottage cheese, but he didn't want to be rude. He said, "Well, I guess so."

"You mean, 'yes, please,' or 'no, thank you'," Mrs. Ames said.

"Yes, please."

"All right. Come on around through the front, then."

"Well, I could come through that hole in the hedge if it's all right."

"All right," Mrs. Ames said, and Jim popped through the bushes. Mrs. Ames said, "Sit over at that little table, and I'll bring out the cottage cheese."

While she was walking toward the house, Jim looked at her clothes to see what was so funny about them. She didn't look too strange to him. She was wearing a raincoat. Of course, it's true it wasn't raining, and it wasn't really cold enough to wear a coat. Oh well, Jim thought, does it really matter? His own grandmother sometimes went around the house in a bathrobe all day.

While he was eating the cottage cheese, Mrs. Ames weeded her garden. When he was finished, he just sat there with nothing to say, but she didn't seem to mind. Finally he said, "That was the best cottage cheese I ever ate."

"I'm glad you liked it," she said.

Jim looked around. "There's a cat I haven't seen before," he said.

"Yes. I've only had him a week. Someone brought him to me. I keep them inside for several days when they're new, so that they'll realize this is their home. This is the first time I've let him out. All my cats are orphans. People find them abandoned, or they have too many, and they bring them to me. I haven't named this one yet. What do you think I should name him?"

Jim looked at the cat. "There really isn't anything very unusual about him," he said.

"No, there isn't. When that's the case, I usually give them ordinary names, like Grace or Henry."

"Golly, do you have cats named Grace and Henry?"

"Yes. And Charles, Steven, Lois, and Genevieve. Why?"

"Well, it just seems funny to give cats people's names. I have an Uncle Henry."

"I have, too," Mrs. Ames said. She smiled. "Of course, we could just name him Leo."

"Yes, I guess we could. I mean, if you like that name."

"Well, many cats are named Leo."

"No, they're not. You're thinking of

lions, and besides, that's not a good reason," Jim said. Suddenly he realized he must have sounded terribly rude. He hadn't meant to, but talking to Mrs. Ames wasn't like talking to a grownup. He looked at her, ready to apologize.

She wasn't angry. She was thinking. "You're right," she said. "Why don't we name him after some friend of yours? Someone you knew before you moved here, perhaps."

"All right," Jim said. "Let's name him Philip Rogers. That's the name of the teacher I had last year."

"Good. Since he's a teacher, we'll call him Mr. Rogers. He does look rather dignified." She stood up and shook the weeds off her coat. "I must cook dinner now."

"Thank you for the cottage cheese," Jim said.

"You're welcome. Goodby," Mrs. Ames said politely. She smiled and went inside.

On the first day of school, Jim and
Jeff and Dave had agreed to walk to
school together. They met at Jim's house,
and when they started off, Baby and Lazy
Grandpa followed them.

"Go home," Jim said. He was worried
about what the cats would do when the
boys crossed the street.

"My gosh, now they're hanging around
you all the time," Jeff said. "Pretty soon
you'll have eighty cats walking you to
school."

"You were probably too nice to them,"
Dave said. "You ought to throw stones
at them; then they won't bother you."
He picked up a stone.

"Hey, don't," Jim said. He turned to
the cats. "Go home," he said crossly.

"Oh well, come on," Dave said.

"I'll have to take them back," Jim said.
"They might get hit by a car."

"We'll be late," Jeff said.

"I'll hurry." Jim picked up the two
cats and ran back to Mrs. Ames' house
with them. He couldn't knock on the

door because his hands were full of cats, so he had to kick it. She took a long time to get to the door. Jim noticed she was still wearing the raincoat.

"You'd better keep them inside," Jim said breathlessly. "They're following the kids to school, and I'm afraid they'll wander out into the street."

"Oh, thank you, Jim. I'm sorry you were inconvenienced."

"It's O.K.," Jim said. He ran back to his friends, and they walked on quickly to school.

"Aren't you scared to go right up to her door like that?" Dave said.

"No, I've talked to her before."

"Yeah? Is she really nuts?"

"Oh, I don't know. She seems all right to me," Jim said.

"I've heard she's pretty mean," Dave said.

Jim didn't think that could be true, but he didn't want to say anything. He didn't want anyone to think he was crazy, too. "We haven't had any trouble yet," he said.

Dave and Jeff both had to go shopping with their mothers that afternoon, so Jim came right home after school. After he'd told his mother about the first day of school, he went out to the back yard to play. He was surprised to hear Billy's voice over in Mrs. Ames' back yard, and when he peeked through the bushes, he saw Billy sitting and eating at the little table. He crawled through the bushes and said, "Hello. How come Billy's over here?"

"This is where the cats live," Billy said.

"Billy doesn't like cottage cheese," Mrs. Ames said. "He doesn't like it with pepper and he doesn't like it with jelly, so I gave him some applesauce. Would you like some, too?"

"Sure," Jim said. "I mean, yes, please."

He was getting used to the way Mrs. Ames talked, not saying hello or what grade are you in.

When she brought the applesauce out, she said, "Mr. Rogers has a sore paw. I don't know how he got it. Are you going to like school?"

"It's all right. How many cats do you have?"

"At the moment I have twenty-seven. Sometimes I have more and sometimes less."

Jim wished he could tell Mrs. Ames that if she had fewer cats, people wouldn't say mean things about her. He said, "Maybe it would be better if you didn't have so many. If you gave them all away except for, say, three, maybe it would... well, maybe it would be better."

Mrs. Ames gave him a funny look. "People have been telling me that for years. But nobody will take care of them if I don't. Of course, everyone thinks I'm very strange because I don't like to see animals die. I probably am."

"Well, I don't care how many cats you have," Jim said.

Billy spoke up. He said, "I don't care how many cats you have, either."

They all laughed. Then Mrs. Ames started telling them what the town was like sixty years ago, when she was a little girl. Billy wandered back into his own yard to play in the sand box, but Jim stayed until dinner time to listen. He liked to try to imagine the town then, with only a few houses and dirt roads. When Mrs. Ames was little, her family used to have picnics where the highway was now, and she had her own horse.

In those days, the town was smaller, and Mrs. Ames had been acquainted with everyone. But a strange thing happened. The more the town grew, the lonelier she became. Her oldest friends died, others moved away, and she had been a widow

for a long time. It didn't really seem like
her town any more, and since she didn't
have children, she didn't find it easy to
get to know new people. Jim could understand that. He knew his mother had
met people at his class tea and at Billy's
nursery school.

All the grownups Jim knew had parties with husbands and wives. Jim could understand that Mrs. Ames might not be invited out very often. And so for years, cats had been Mrs. Ames' best company. At first it hadn't mattered to anyone, because there weren't as many houses on the street. But now the street was full of strangers, and they all found the cats a nuisance.

Jim's mother already knew half the women on the block, and he was trying to think how Mrs. Ames could get to know them. But he couldn't really imagine her sitting with his mother and her friends, drinking coffee and talking about children. Finally Jim said to her, "You ought to come over and tell my mother how to make cottage cheese."

But Mrs. Ames just smiled, and then Jim heard his mother calling him to come in for dinner.

At dinner that night, Jim said to his father, "I don't think Mrs. Ames is crazy. She's really O.K."

"Well, you can certainly be different without being crazy," Jim's father said. "The only thing is, it's better to be different in a way that doesn't disturb people. Now, if Mrs. Ames collected goldfish instead of cats, nobody would think much of it."

"But she feels sorry for the cats. They'd all die if she didn't take care of them."

"But you have to admit it isn't fair," Jim's father said. "What would happen if everyone had that many cats?"

Jim smiled. "I guess we'd be up to our necks in cats."

"Yes," his father said. "That's why we

have an SPCA, which is the Society for the Prevention of Cruelty to Animals. They take care of the strays. She doesn't have to be the one to do it."

"But she said they'd die if she didn't!"

"Well, the SPCA puts them to sleep. That's much kinder than letting them starve."

"But putting them to sleep means killing them, really, doesn't it?"

"Yes," his father said. "But it is more cruel to let them starve than to put a painless end to them."

"Well, she just doesn't see it that way," Jim said.

After that, nobody said anything about Mrs. Ames and her cats for several weeks. It was getting dark earlier, and the boys didn't play after dinner any more. One day Mrs. Ames called to him from her side of the hedge and asked him to get a book from the library for her, and she paid him for doing the errand. After that,

whenever he needed money, he would stop to see if she had a job for him. Quite often, she would ask him to do something—get a log from the woodpile, or pick up something at the drugstore.

Whenever Dave and Jeff found out that Jim had done an errand for Mrs. Ames, they kidded him about it, so he stopped mentioning it. "Are you working for the cat lady again?" they'd say. "Pretty soon you'll grow pointed ears and a long tail."

Then something happened. On the way to school one morning, Jeff said, "Did you hear what happened to Mrs. Bolton?"

Jim knew that Mrs. Bolton lived on the other side of Mrs. Ames. "What happened?"

"One of the cat lady's cats tripped her, and she sprained her ankle."

Jim could tell from looking at Dave and Jeff that they thought this was somehow Mrs. Ames' fault. "It's not such a big deal to sprain your ankle," Jim said. "Why didn't she look where she was going?"

"She couldn't," Dave said. "She was

carrying her baby, and she couldn't see the cat under her feet. And when she fell she was trying to keep her baby from getting hurt."

"Oh," Jim said, and suddenly he felt very sad. He was sad about Mrs. Bolton, and about Mrs. Ames, too, and about the trouble he was sure there was going to be.

"Mr. Bolton is starting a petition to get rid of the cats," Jeff said. "I'll bet everyone will sign it, too. My father says it's bad enough to have them killing birds and howling, but this is really serious. He says it's too bad people always wait for someone to get hurt before something is done."

Jim only nodded, although he thought what Jeff's Dad had said was pretty silly. After all, cats didn't ordinarily hurt anyone. But the boys were looking at him, so he didn't say anything.

Jim thought about the accident and the petition all day. After school he went right home and said to his mother, "Have you heard anything about a petition to get rid of Mrs. Ames' cats?"

"Yes. Mr. Bolton went to every house on the street last night to get names. He was here after you were asleep."

"Did you and Dad sign your names?"

"Yes. We felt we had to."

"Oh," Jim said. He went up to his room.

"Jim," his mother called, "don't you want a snack?"

"No, thanks," Jim said.

"Don't you feel well?" she asked.

"It's not that," Jim said, and he closed the door to his room. He wanted to talk to his father when he came home. He did his homework, but he was so upset at his parents for signing the petition that he couldn't read his library book. He sat waiting to hear the front door close, because that would mean his father had come home.

Jim went right downstairs, and he didn't even wait for his father to take off his coat. He said, "Why did you and Mom sign that petition?"

"Because I thought it was the right thing to do," his father said. "I think it's important to get rid of those cats. She doesn't have to get rid of every single one, you know, only twenty-five or -six." He smiled, but Jim didn't smile back. They went and sat down in the living room. His mother came in, too, and sat down with them. Billy came in and hugged his father, so that Jim had to wait a few minutes until he left before saying what he wanted to say.

"Signing that petition was just like saying Mrs. Ames' cats should be taken

away from her and killed. That's what it really means," Jim said.

His father said, "Mrs. Ames likes her cats, but to everyone else on the street— maybe a hundred people—they are a big nuisance. Is that fair?"

"I know all about them killing birds, and the garbage, and the howling at night," Jim said, "and I still don't think they're such a nuisance that anyone has the right to take them away from her."

"That's what you think, and that's what she thinks. But many other people think she has no right to bother others like that. And the Board of Health considers it a health hazard to keep too many pets."

"I don't know what will happen to Mrs. Ames if they take away her cats," Jim said. "They're all she has for company."

"I don't understand why she can't find some friends for company," Jim's mother said. "They say she's lived here all her life. She's certainly had time to make friends, but she's not a bit friendly."

"Well, it may not be that. It may be that she's shy," Jim's father said. "It's just the number of cats that bothers me."

"How do they kill them?" Jim asked.

"They put them in a gas chamber. They feel no pain at all. There are too many cats in the world, Jim, and some people turn them loose to starve to death. Some people drown them. Is that kinder than putting them in a gas chamber?"

"In school we're learning that pretty soon there will be too many people in the world," Jim said. "Are we going to put them in a gas chamber, too?"

"Oh, come now," his father said. "People are more important than cats."

"Not to Mrs. Ames," Jim said.

"But that's her own fault!" Jim's mother said.

Jim stood up. There didn't seem to be any use in talking any more. "I'm going out for a little while," he said.

"It's dark. Don't go too far away," his mother said.

While he was putting on his coat, he heard his mother say, "Well, whatever other complaints there are about those cats, they have this family upset."

"Have you finished your homework?" his father called out.

"Yes."

"Please don't be out more than twenty minutes," he said. "It's getting late."

"O.K.," Jim said. He went outside and stood thinking for a few minutes, and then he crawled through the bushes and went over to Mrs. Ames' back door.

She looked surprised when she finally opened the door. "Why, hello, Jim," she said.

"Hello," Jim said. "Listen, Mrs. Ames, you have to invite me inside because I have to talk to you. I'm sorry."

Mrs. Ames looked even more surprised. "I never invite anyone in. I'll put on my coat and come outside."

"No," Jim said. "People could see us, or hear us talking, and it's important. I'll have to come in."

Mrs. Ames stared at him as though she didn't know what to do, but she finally opened the door and they went inside. It was easy to understand why she never let anyone in. There were cats everywhere and the place was a mess. They sat down at the kitchen table, and Jim said, "Did you know there's a petition going around to get rid of your cats?"

Mrs. Ames shook her head. "No, I didn't," she said. "Since Mrs. Bolton's accident, I've been trying to keep them all inside. I really didn't think people would go this far. As if I were guilty of some crime!" She started to cry.

Jim was miserable. She said, "I've always tried to keep them in my own yard, but of course a few are bound to get out."

"Listen," Jim said, "the reason I wanted to talk to you is that I'm going to do something. I didn't want you to do anything before I have a chance to see what I can do."

Mrs. Ames shook her head. "You can't stop them, Jim," she said. "They've been wanting to do this for a long time. Nobody could think of a really good reason for me to give up my cats, you see, because there really isn't a very good reason.

I've heard people say the cats get into garbage, but they don't if you have the lid on tight. People should have the lids on tight on their garbage cans anyway. Cats don't bark—like dogs, and they're not nearly as destructive as children. It isn't that I don't like dogs or children, Jim. But I don't have any. Now they think they've found a good reason to take the cats away. You'll never stop them."

"I wasn't thinking of trying to stop them," Jim said. "There wouldn't be any use in that. But there's something I have to find out. O.K.?"

"O.K.," Mrs. Ames said. She still didn't look very happy, but she smiled at him when he left.

Jim had several errands to do the next day before he could go back to Mrs. Ames and tell her his plan. The next afternoon after school, he dropped his books at home and went right down to the Town Hall. He had a terrible time finding the right person to talk to, but finally he got all the information that he needed.

By that time it was too late to do anything else, so he had to put off his other errands until the next day, which was Saturday. He had planned to play football with Dave and Jeff, but he called them and told them he was busy. He started out in the morning and didn't finish doing all he'd planned until five o'clock. Then he went to Mrs. Ames' house. This time she opened the door and let him in.

He handed her a piece of paper. "You'll have to fill this out and send it right in," he said. "It's an application for a kennel license. I found out this street isn't zoned against kennels. The petition is going to be taken up in two weeks. But if you have a kennel going by then, and your application is already on file, you'll be ready for the inspectors when they come. And then there won't be anything they can do."

Mrs. Ames looked at him for a long time. Then she said, "Would you like some coffee?"

"Coffee?" Jim said. Nobody had ever offered Jim coffee before. "Sure, I'll try it. Yes, please."

She poured coffee with milk and sugar for both of them, and then sat down. "Jim," she said, "I don't see how I can have a kennel going in two weeks."

"I'm going to build it," Jim said. "I found out what the requirements are. With six cats in a cage, five big cages would be enough. I'm sure I can make cages. I have all the instructions, and they don't sound too hard. Last year I made a go-cart, and that's much harder."

"Where are you going to get the materials? It sounds rather expensive, and I don't have very much money."

"I've already got about half, and I'm getting the other half in a few days."

"Really? How on earth did you do that?"

"Well, I got a lot of scraps at the lumber yard. I used to get stuff at the lumber yard where I lived before, so I thought I might as well try the same thing here, and it worked. And then there's a machine shop on the edge of town. I got some old hinges there. My biggest break was the screens. I talked to some guys who are tearing down an old screened porch, and the owner is willing to let me take all the screens. And there are still more places to go if I have to. I could go to the junk yard and the liquor store."

"The liquor store?"

"Yes. There's one kind of whiskey that still comes in wooden crates. The others switched to cardboard." Seeing the look on Mrs. Ames' face, he said, "The reason I know is that I've been building things a long time, and I've been looking for junk as long as I can remember. One of the first things my Dad did when we moved in here was to set up a workshop for us in the cellar."

"Well," Mrs. Ames said. "Well, well, well."

"So you mail in that form," Jim said, "and I'll get started on the cages."

"You know," Mrs. Ames said, "I'm not the only person in the neighborhood with cats. I don't think anything would have happened if it had been someone else's cat Mrs. Bolton tripped over. It really doesn't seem fair, does it?"

"No," Jim said. He started to leave.

Mrs. Ames said, "Jim, do you really think you can build five cages in two weeks?"

That had been bothering Jim. The truth of the matter was that he didn't see how he could possibly build five cages in two weeks, but he was going to try. "Sure I can," he said.

Mrs. Ames smiled and said, "Well, thank you. I hope this works out."

When he left, Jim thought, my gosh, in some ways she's just like Billy. You tell them you can do something, and they both believe you really can do it.

The next week, when Dave and Jeff came to pick him up after school, he told them he couldn't play because he was working on something.

"What?" Jeff asked.

"Oh, a thing I'm building."

"What kind of thing?" Dave asked.

"A wooden thing," Jim said.

"What's it going to be used for?" Jeff asked.

Jim thought about that. He said, "Well, for storage." And that's all he would say.

The only trouble was that the job wasn't going very fast. It wasn't even going as fast as he'd hoped. He made quite a few mistakes on the first cage. He had never worked with screening

before, and it was hard to get it tight
enough. Even after he had the work fig-
ured out, and could see that the others
would go faster, he hadn't finished the
first cage at the end of the week. Then

he began to wonder if the cages would really pass the inspection, if there was room for them in Mrs. Ames' house, and if the cats would claw right through them.

He had other problems, too. His parents knew he was spending all his free time building something, but he hadn't told them what it was, and he was afraid there would be another argument if they insisted on knowing what he was making. Then, too, he was worried about Dave and Jeff. With homework and his project, he had no time at all to play with them, and he was afraid they wouldn't want to play with him any more when he was finished. They would think he was nutty if they found out what he was doing.

By the middle of the second week, things began to get worse. Jim was walking home from school with his friends, and Dave said, "I guess you can't play again today."

"I'll be finished with this job soon, and then I'll play," Jim said.

"That must be some job," Jeff said. "And you won't even tell us what it is. It sure looks as if you'd rather work down there in the basement than play with us any more."

"It's not that," Jim said. He was just about to say he'd take the day off and play with them, but they ran on ahead to catch up with some other boys.

Jim went straight home and did his homework. He had a lot that day, so he couldn't start to work on the cages until after dinner. But when he started down the basement stairs, his father called, "Come on in the living room a minute, will you, Jim?"

Jim went in and sat down with his parents. His father said, "Jim, what is this project you're working on?"

By this time, Jim was feeling so bad that he didn't even try to fool his father.

He said, "I'm working on cages. I'm making them for Mrs. Ames so she can have a kennel."

His mother said, "A kennel!"

"Gee whiz," Jim said, "can't I do what I want? Do we have to have another big, long discussion?"

"I thought that was it," his father said. "I don't believe you've thought this through. What do you think it's going to be like—living next door to a kennel?"

"There's no law against it. I checked," Jim said.

"Wait a minute," Jim's mother said. "I'm sorry, but this is where I put my foot down. I signed the petition because I thought it was the right thing to do, but I like cats and I can't stand the idea of putting them in cages. It's too cruel. Cats were never meant to live in cages, and they would be miserable."

By then, Jim felt as though everything had gone completely wrong. He shouted,

"Oh, forget the whole thing!" and ran
upstairs to his room. He lay down on his
bed and tried to think. It hadn't occurred
to him that it would be unkind to keep
the cats in the cages, but the minute his

mother mentioned it, he knew she was right. He wondered why Mrs. Ames had agreed. Maybe she wouldn't really keep them in the cages, except for the inspection, but that would be cheating. And then Jim had another awful idea. How could anyone be sure Mrs. Ames would only keep enough cats for the cages? If nobody had ever been able to tell Mrs. Ames to keep only two or three cats, how could he tell her to keep only thirty? He lay there thinking for a long time, and then his mother called, "Jim, may I come in?"

"Yes," Jim said, "but I don't want to talk about the cat business any more."

"No, but I've had an idea," his mother said. "Tomorrow after school why don't we take a drive over to the animal shelter? There's one about fifteen miles from here."

"What good would that do?" Jim asked.

"I don't know," his mother said. "But taking care of stray animals is their business, and since you've gotten interested in this problem, you might be able to learn something that would help you."

"Well, all right," Jim said. He was sure it wouldn't help to visit the animal shelter, but he knew his mother was trying to make him feel better, so he agreed. Finally, he went to sleep.

As soon as they drove in the driveway at the shelter, they heard the dogs barking. They made so much noise Jim had trouble hearing his mother when she said, "You go on in and talk to the people. Billy and I will walk around and look at the animals."

Jim got out and started toward the main building. He passed the big cages where the dogs were. There were dogs of all kinds and sizes and colors, and it seemed as though every single one was barking. Then he went into the office building, where it was quieter, and saw a lady sitting behind a desk. She smiled and said, "May I help you?"

"Yes," Jim said. "I wanted to ask you some questions."

"All right," the lady said.

It was hard to know where to begin. Finally, Jim said, "If somebody brought a whole bunch of cats in here, what would happen to them?"

"Well, we would try very hard to find homes for them. It's one of our main jobs. We put ads in the newspaper, and we advertise on the radio."

"What will happen if you can't find homes for them?" Jim asked.

"Well, you see, we are allowed by law to keep only a certain number of animals. We have space and money to care for a limited number, so when we can't find homes, we have to put them to sleep."

"Are there really that many cats that nobody can take care of?"

"Oh, yes," the lady said. "Here at this shelter, we all love animals. But we are forced to put almost five hundred cats to sleep every month."

"My gosh," Jim said.

"Yes," the lady said. "Of course, it's much kinder than letting them starve in the streets."

"I guess that's really all I wanted to know," Jim said.

"Would you like to look around?"

"All right," Jim said.

Jim looked at the animals. There was a rabbit he would have liked to take home, but he didn't think this was a very good time to ask his mother about it.

On the way home, Billy kept asking if he could have a cat, and Jim and his mother just looked at each other and laughed.

When they got home, Jim said, "I guess I'd better go over and talk to Mrs. Ames."

"What will you say to her?" his mother asked.

"I have to tell her it won't work to put her cats in cages," Jim said. "Then she'll probably cry. Holy Cow!"

"Listen, Jim, would you like me to invite her over here? Maybe it would be easier if you broke the news to her right here. And maybe if she got to feel that she knew some families in the neighborhood, the cats wouldn't seem so important to her."

"Well, you could try it."

Jim sat with his mother while she made the telephone call, but he could tell that Mrs. Ames had refused the invitation. "Why wouldn't she come?" he asked, after his mother had hung up.

"She said she's not dressed."

"She's never dressed," Jim said. "She wears a raincoat all the time."

"It's sad," his mother said, but for some reason they both started to laugh.

"Well, I'm going to go get it over with," Jim said.

This time, Mrs. Ames answered the door right away and asked him in. She said, "Your mother called to ask if I would come over and have coffee with her. Wasn't that nice?"

"You should have gone," Jim said.

Mrs. Ames shook her head. "I never accept invitations. If I did, I would have to repay someone with an invitation here, and I can't have anyone come in, because they are critical of my cats."

"That's dumb," Jim said. When he was with Mrs. Ames, he kept forgetting she was really a grownup. "Excuse me, but it's silly not to get to know people, Mrs. Ames."

"Well, you can't very well go to someone else's house and then never ask them to your house."

"But Billy and I have been here lots of times," Jim said. He was almost shouting.

"Well, yes, that's true. I hadn't thought of that."

"Anyway, I'm not here to talk about that," Jim said. "What I wanted to say is, I don't think it will work to keep the cats in cages."

"Well, no, not permanently. It would just be temporary."

"You mean, you'd just put them in the cages long enough for the inspector to see them, and then let them out again?"

Mrs. Ames looked at him earnestly. "Wasn't that what you found out, Jim? The inspectors have to see them in cages. Wasn't that it?"

"Yes," Jim said. "But can't you see? If

you don't really keep them in the cages, you'll be breaking the law."

But when he looked at Mrs. Ames, he felt sure nobody would ever be able to explain the law to her. She said, "But it wouldn't be fair to the cats to keep them in cages, Jim."

"I know," Jim said. "That's why I had to stop making them."

"I'm sorry you had to put in so much time," she said.

"Couldn't you give just a few to the animal shelter?" Jim asked. "I went over there, and it's not so bad."

"You're not being honest," Mrs. Ames said. "What you mean is, why don't I have some of my cats done away with. No, I can't do that."

"What will you tell the inspectors?" Jim asked.

"I'll have to tell them I only have four or five," Mrs. Ames said.

Jim looked at Mrs. Ames. He was

thinking, now who's not being honest? But he knew it wouldn't do any good to say that. So he just said, "Well, I hope everything turns out all right."

"You've been very nice, Jim," Mrs. Ames said.

A few minutes later, Jim went home. Mrs. Ames hadn't been upset after all. She must have decided she could fool the inspectors and keep all her cats. There wasn't anything else he could do about the cats. Now, all he wanted to do was to call Dave and Jeff and start playing with them again.

Jim told Dave and Jeff he wanted them to come to his house the next day. His mother made cookies, to help everyone get on better terms again, and after the snack, Jim took his friends down into the basement. He showed them the cages.

"This is what I was working so hard on," he said. "I was thinking of going into the kennel business, but after I looked into it, I decided it wouldn't work."

Dave and Jeff looked at all the cages. "Well," Dave said, "now it looks as if you're going to have to go into the cage business."

They all laughed, and Jim suggested they be partners. For the next few weeks the three boys finished the cages and

started selling them. They made a little
money for Christmas, and that made Jim
feel a lot better about all the work he'd
put in on the cages. But he was still
thinking about Mrs. Ames and her cats.

He wondered what would happen to Linda and Lazy Grandpa and Mr. Rogers if the inspectors took her cats away. Every few days, he went over to ask her if the inspectors had been there yet, but they hadn't.

Finally it got to be Christmas. Jim's mother asked him if he'd like to invite Mrs. Ames to Christmas dinner, and she accepted. She brought a fruit cake, and didn't talk about cats, and even Jim's father seemed to enjoy hearing her talk about how the town was in the old days. Before she left, Jim asked her again what had happened.

"Did the inspectors ever come?"

"Oh, yes. They told me there was a law against keeping more than five cats," Mrs. Ames said. She smiled.

Jim didn't have to ask her what she was going to do. He knew she wasn't going to do anything. It would probably be months before anyone complained

again, and perhaps they wouldn't com-
plain at all. If they did, the whole thing
would start all over.

A few days after Christmas, Mrs. Ames

telephoned Jim. She said, "I thought you might be interested to know that I'm not taking any more cats. Someone brought me another cat, and I told him to take it to the SPCA. Now that I keep them indoors I find I have too many."

"I think you did the right thing," Jim said. "I think you had to do that."

"I wanted you to know," Mrs. Ames said. "You were the only one who tried to help me."

"Well, you just had to stop sometime," Jim said again.

"Yes. When it snows, will you shovel my sidewalk?"

"Sure," Jim said, and he smiled. She sounded like herself again, saying things when you didn't expect them.

"I'd be willing to give away two or three more, Jim, if I were sure of a really good home for them. And Linda is going to have kittens. Do you know anyone who might want one of her kittens?"

"I might," Jim said. "I'll let you know."

When he hung up, Jim went into the living room to tell his parents. He said, "Guess what? Mrs. Ames isn't taking any more cats. Someone tried to give her another one and she told him to take it to the SPCA."

"Well!" Jim's father said. "That's quite a victory. You have more influence than anyone else in this neighborhood, I guess."

"It's because you were helpful and friendly. She's trying her best to do what she knows is right. She didn't have any reason to try before," Jim's mother said.

"Well, I learned one thing," Jim said. "Sometimes it takes a whole lot of time and work just to change things a little bit. Now she's even willing to give away a couple of cats, and if I can find homes for Linda's kittens, that will be a help, too."

Just then, Billy came in. He said, "There's something I wanted for Christmas that I didn't get. A kitten!"

"I think I know where we might find one, Billy," said his father. "Don't you, Jim?"

Jim laughed and then he said, "I have a funny feeling that I'm not going to have any trouble at all finding homes for Linda's kittens."

And he was right.